Piper's Night Before Christmas

by
Mark Lowry and Martha Bolton

Illustrated by Kristen Myers

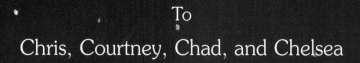

To

Chris, Courtney, Chad, and Chelsea

my nieces and nephews—
not a hyper one in the bunch

Our purpose at Howard Publishing is to:
- *Increase faith* in the hearts of growing Christians
- *Inspire holiness* in the lives of believers
- *Instill hope* in the hearts of struggling people everywhere

Because He's coming again!

Piper's Night Before Christmas © 1998 by Mark Lowry
All rights reserved. Printed in the United States of America
Published by Howard Publishing Co., Inc.,
3117 North 7th Street, West Monroe, Louisiana 71291-2227

98 99 00 01 02 03 04 05 06 07   10 9 8 7 6 5 4 3 2

Library of Congress Cataloging-in-Publication Data
Lowry, Mark.
    Piper's night before Christmas / Mark Lowry and Martha Bolton ; illustrated by Kristen Myers.
        p.   cm.
        Summary: On Christmas Eve, Piper the hyper mouse discovers that it is better to give than to receive.
    ISBN 1-58229-000-8
    [1. Christmas—Fiction. 2. Mice—Fiction. 3. Stories in rhyme.] I. Bolton, Martha, 1951- . II. Myers, Kristen, ill. III. Title. IV. Title: Night before Christmas.
    PZ8.3.L9556Pi 1998
    [Fic]—dc21
                                                                                                    98-42458
                                                                                                    CIP
                                                                                                    AC
Digital Enhancement by Suzanne Floyd, LinDee Loveland, and Vanessa Bearden

They said . . .
It was the night before Christmas,
And all through the house,
Not a creature was stirring—
Not even a mouse.

But hours before,
There was much stirring then,
For Piper the Mouse
Was the hyperist he'd been!

He'd tried to be good,
But his patience grew thin.
He wanted it Christmas
Right there and right then!

He'd stared at those presents
Like catfish to bait.
What was inside them?
He just couldn't wait!

One gift was marked "Piper,"
So trying to peek,
He pulled on the ribbon,
Stretching it with his feet.

But instead of it breaking,
It SNAPPED! with a force,
Catapulting poor Piper
In the air, and of course,
The window was open,
So out Piper flew . . .

There's no telling how many red lights he went through!

Some church doors were open;
He flew right inside—
Past the pews and the pastor—
What a wonderful ride!

Piper landed smack-dab
In a pillow of hay,
Then realized he was now
In their Christmas Eve play!

There was Mary and Joseph
And the shepherds and sheep.
They were saying their lines.
He didn't dare make a peep.

They said that God loved us
And gave us His son;
So at Christmas it's giving,
Not getting, that's fun!

Piper looked right beside him,
And there on the hay

Lay the most precious baby
Ever born to this day.

Piper jumped off that manger
And ran to his house,
Breaking all the speed limits
That apply to a mouse.

He got his one present
And dragged it four miles . . .

To the church . . .

To the stage . . .

To the manger,
and smiled.

He gave it to Jesus.
It was all he could do.

Then the angel said,
"Jesus would rather have YOU!"

The play was now over.
The cast took their bows.
Piper took one himself
With the sheep and the cows.

Then he walked home that night
With something new to believe,
For he'd learned it's much better
To give than receive.

When he got to his house,
He did not make a peep,
Just made gifts for his loved ones,
Then he fell fast asleep.

So that night before Christmas,
That's why all through the house,
Not a creature was stirring,
Not even Piper the Mouse!